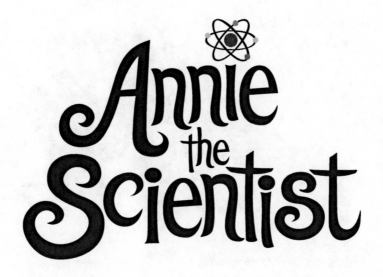

Annie the Scientist

written by
Daniel Johnson

illustrations by
Lynn Alpert

Pass Christian, MS

To Anna, for her enthusiasm –DJ

To Natalie and Jules,
my muses –LA

Annie the Scientist
Text copyright © Daniel Johnson, 2013
Illustrations copyright © Lynn Alpert, 2013
All Rights Reserved

For information about permission to reproduce selections
from this book, please visit the Character Publishing website.
www.CharacterPublishing.org

Library of Congress Cataloging-in-Publication Data
Johnson, Daniel.
Annie the Scientist/written by Daniel Johnson

Summary: Annie the Scientist is a 6.14 X 9.21 hardback
chapter book about a gifted child who, despite her doubting
friends, insists that she is a scientist. Annie simply refuses
to see life's ordinary events as anything but extraordinary.
[Children's – Fiction. 2. Science]
ISBN: 978-0-9890797-3-0

Library of Congress Control Number   2013934141

Designed by Lynn Alpert
First Edition Edited by Brie Ishee
Proudly Printed in the United States of America

*"The knowledge we have of things is small indeed,
while that of which we are ignorant is immense."*

-Pierre Simon Laplace (1749-1827)

1.
A New Girl

One morning last spring, on a day that was sunny-but-not-hot, with a sky that was cloudy-but-still-blue, a new girl moved into our neighborhood. Her name was Annie. She had brown hair. And she was a scientist.

This is how it started. On that first day, Annie was sitting outside in the backyard, holding a garden hose. She was staring at the hose – staring at it as if it were something really special. But it wasn't. It was just a hose.

"Hi, there," we all said.

"Hi, there," said Annie, not looking up.

"What are you doing?" we inquired.

"Watch," Annie replied. "If you just let the water come out all by itself, it flows slowly to the ground. But," she said " – if I put my thumb over the end..."

Annie squeezed the end of the hose hard with her

1

thumb. The water started shooting out much faster – and much farther. When her thumb was on the hose, Annie could shoot the water almost all the way across the yard.

We stood and watched. We looked at each other. This girl was odd.

"Why," we asked, "are you playing with a hose?"

"Oh, I study things," said Annie. "And I think about things. I'm a scientist."

We all laughed. This girl wasn't a scientist. Scientists were grown-up people who walked around inside a laboratory, wore white coats, and worked with chemicals and microscopes. Scientists were not kids who stood in the backyard with a drippy garden hose.

"What's your name?" we asked Annie.

"Annie," she said.

"What good is playing with a hose to a 'scientist'?" we asked.

Annie Annie smiled and shrugged her shoulders. "I just want to learn how things work. Big things, little things – even things that seem so normal you don't think about them. I saw the hose, and I said, 'I want to understand this thing.' If you learn all you can about one thing, sometimes you can use it to understand other things."

We didn't say anything. This Annie girl was just plain weird. She just kept looking at the water coming out of the hose, and she kept adjusting the pressure with her thumb.

Finally, we said, "Annie, you are not a scientist. NO KID CAN BE A SCIENTIST."

Annie shrugged. "Oh, I certainly am a scientist."

Right then, we were certain Annie was just being silly. And goofy.

But eventually, Annie changed our minds.

It didn't happen right away – it happened slowly.

It took a whole year.

And this – this! – is the story of how Annie became a scientist.

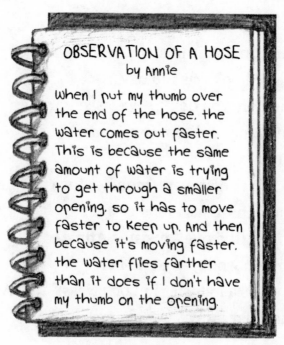

OBSERVATION OF A HOSE
by Annie

When I put my thumb over the end of the hose, the water comes out faster. This is because the same amount of water is trying to get through a smaller opening, so it has to move faster to keep up. And then because it's moving faster, the water flies farther than it does if I don't have my thumb on the opening.

2.
Annie Discovers a Monster

MICROGRAPHIA:
(Or, some Physiological Descriptions of Minute
Bodies made by Magnifying Glasses with
Observations and Inquires Thereupon)
-Robert Hooke, 1665

The very next day, Annie decided to discover a monster.

We came by to see if she wanted to jump rope. She was sitting on the front steps, reading a thick book. The name of the book was Biology.

"What are you doing?" we asked Annie.

"I'm going to discover a monster," said Annie, not looking up.

"You can't discover a monster," we told her. "There are no such things as monsters."

"Oh, I'll find one," insisted Annie.

"No, you won't," we told her.

"There is a monster in Loch Ness," said Annie.

"That's far away," we told her.

"Some people say there are monsters in the wilderness of Canada," said Annie.

"We're not in the wilderness of Canada, Annie," we said. "You may read big books, and you may study hoses, but you're wrong about this. There are no monsters here."

Annie smiled, except you couldn't see her face from behind the book, just her eyes. But her eyes were smiling, somehow – twinkling, with little laugh lines pointing upwards. "Come back tomorrow," she said. "I'll show you then."

* * *

The next day, Annie was outside standing in the driveway. She was walking around with a tape measure.

"Find any monsters?" we asked.

Annie didn't answer. She was writing something down in her little red notebook.

"What are you doing?" we asked.

"Looking for a place where monsters will want to live."

"Annie – THERE ARE NO SUCH THINGS AS MONSTERS," we said.

Annie smiled.

She walked up and down the driveway. Every once in a while, she would stop near a slight dip in the ground. Each time she did this, she lowered the tape measure down into the dip. Then she wrote down the number in

5

the notebook.

"One inch," said Annie. "I need a place deeper than that."

"Annie, this is so silly," we told her.

"Oh, this is definitely not silly," insisted Annie.

Finally, she found a place that was deep enough to satisfy her. "Three inches," she said. She marked the spot with a little stick. Then she stood up and spread her arms. "My friends," she said deeply, "this is where I will find a monster."

"When?" we all asked.

"On Friday."

It was Monday now. We couldn't help wondering, What will happen in four days to make Annie find a monster?

* * *

On Tuesday, nothing happened. Annie didn't come outside. She stayed indoors all day and organized her geology samples. "With enough pressure, limestone becomes marble!" she told us.

On Wednesday, still nothing happened. Annie came outside, but all she did was watch butterflies. "Why butterflies?" asked Macy Fillmore.

"I like butterflies," said Annie.

On Thursday, it rained all day. It rained so hard that nobody played outside at all. Finally, around three o'clock, the rain stopped, and it became hot and sunny.

On Friday afternoon, it was still hot and sunny. We all ran to Annie's house to see about her 'monsters.'

Annie was in the driveway. She was wearing yellow rubber boots that said, "I ♥ Protein Molecules" on them. She was kneeling down, looking at the place she had marked earlier in the week.

Except now, the little dip was a little mud puddle.

"So, Annie," we demanded, "where are your 'monsters'?"

Annie pointed at the puddle. "In here. I am sure there will be some monsters living here."

We looked down. The puddle was tiny. And gross. "Annie," we said, "that is a mud puddle."

"That," said Annie, "is a monster hideout." She reached into her pocket and pulled out a test tube.

"Where did you get the test tube?" we asked.

"For Christmas," Annie answered. She bent down. Carefully, slowly, she lowered the test tube to the mud puddle. We all watched.

Carefully, slowly, she dipped the test tube into the water. ("Gross," said Kyle Materson.)

And carefully, slowly, Annie filled the test-tube with mud-water! Then she lifted it back out and put on the cap.

"Now, I have my monsters!" said Annie.

"WHAT?" we all screamed. "YOU DON'T HAVE ANY MONSTERS! ALL YOU HAVE IS MUD!"

"To the lab!" Annie cried, pumping her fist into the air.

Of course we had to follow. Nobody believed Annie – exactly – but nobody wanted to miss out on what was going to happen. Annie led us around to the back of the house. "You'll have to take off those muddy shoes," she told us.

Inside, she took us to a dusky room with lots of papers taped to the wall. "This is my lab," said Annie. Some of the papers were pictures and drawings of nature like flowers and bugs. Others had words on them describing things she had studied like a cloud or her garden hose.

Over in a corner of the room was a microscope covered by a dust cloth. Annie whipped off the cover and turned on the machine.

We had to ask: "Annie, where ON EARTH did you get a microscope?"

"For my birthday," said Annie. "Now, to examine the sample," she added dramatically.

Once again, Annie worked carefully and slowly. She poured a drop – just a tiny drop – of mud-water onto the microscope. Then she whirled a few dials and looked through.

Nothing happened.

Annie waited, her eyes staring through the microscope.

We waited.

The whole world waited.

The clock ticked.

We held our breath.

Finally –

"Here are the monsters."

We took turns peering into the microscope. We gasped. Swimming around in the drop of water were dozens of squiggly, squirmy, swimming, ugly creatures! Monsters!

"Look at that!"

"Wow!"

"Real monsters!"

"How did you know, Annie?"

Annie smiled. "Those are microorganisms. They're invisible – except with a microscope. They swim around in the mud. Some of them only have one cell."

"Weird!" we all exclaimed.

"Robert Hooke would be so pleased," said Annie.

We looked at each other. We looked at Annie. "Who," we said, "is Robert Hooke?"

"Oh, never mind," said Annie.

Amy Sheldon was skeptical. "Those aren't monsters," she announced, looking up from her turn at the microscope. "Those are specks of darker-colored mud."

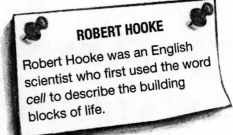

ROBERT HOOKE

Robert Hooke was an English scientist who first used the word *cell* to describe the building blocks of life.

"No," said Annie, "they're not. The specks of mud don't move, but the living creatures swim around."

We looked again. Sure enough, Annie was right.

Annie carefully and slowly pushed us away from the microscope.

"Monsters are everywhere – if you just look close enough."

We all left Annie's house that afternoon thinking, What an interesting idea!

"Do you think she really is a scientist?" asked Mary Ann Louis.

We all thought it over. Finally, Amy turned her nose in the air and said, "Naw. Looking at some bugs in the mud doesn't make you a scientist. She's gonna have to do something better than that to make me believe her..."

We agreed. Annie was clever, but she was going to have to be more impressive than that. Little did we know, she was already working on it.

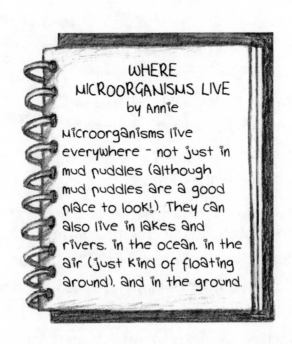

WHERE MICROORGANISMS LIVE
by Annie

Microorganisms live everywhere - not just in mud puddles (although mud puddles are a good place to look!). They can also live in lakes and rivers, in the ocean, in the air (just kind of floating around), and in the ground.

3.
Magnetic Levitation

"What a stunning and unexpected conclusion!
How elegant the proof!"
-Carl Sagan, *Cosmos,* 1980

One afternoon, as a soft breeze was clinking the wind chimes, we all sat around Annie's porch, having a snack. Mary Ann was eating crackers-and-cheese; Annie was eating a pear and reading a book called The Earth: Our Planet; and Oliver Sloane was twisting apart his Oreos to eat the inside first.

"You'll never guess what I saw last night!" he said, licking out the cream. "My dad took me to see this magician guy – and he made a lady float in the air!"

We all agreed, that would be something to see.

Oliver went on. "The magician called it lev... levi...lev..."

"Levitation," said Annie, not looking up from the book she was reading.

"Yeah!" said Oliver, "Levitation. Of course afterwards

the magician showed how it really worked, and it wasn't magic at all. He had the supports hidden by the curtain. Nothing can just float in the air like that."

We all agreed nothing could just float by itself. Then Annie spoke up.

"Actually," she said, looking up, "the Earth floats on nothing." She opened her book and showed us a big picture taken from space, showing the whole planet Earth just sitting there in the blackness, hanging on nothing.

We frowned. That wasn't a fair comparison. "Okay, Annie," we said. "THE EARTH DOESN'T COUNT. We're talking about regular, everyday stuff."

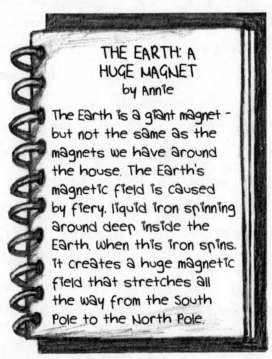

THE EARTH: A HUGE MAGNET
by Annie

The Earth is a giant magnet - but not the same as the magnets we have around the house. The Earth's magnetic field is caused by fiery, liquid iron spinning around deep inside the Earth. When this iron spins, it creates a huge magnetic field that stretches all the way from the South Pole to the North Pole.

Annie giggled. "Balloons float," she said, "if they are filled with hot air or helium."

We all looked at each other. Annie wasn't playing properly. "Okay," we said. "BESIDES the Earth and BESIDES balloons, NOTHING CAN JUST FLOAT."

"Bubbles?" asked Annie, smiling softly.

We didn't say anything.

"I know what you mean," said Annie, putting down the book and stretching out on the porch stairs. "You're talking about heavy stuff. Regular, clunky, heavy stuff – like a rock, or a television."

We smiled. Annie finally understood. "Exactly," we said.

Suddenly, Annie sat up. "How about a small piece of metal?" she asked. "Would you say that a small piece of metal cannot float in the air?"

We all looked at each other. No one could think of any reason a small piece of metal should float in the air.

"Um, no," we said. "A small piece of metal cannot float."

Annie smiled. She stood up. "Wait here," she told us, and ran into the house.

We waited. What in the world was Annie going to do this time?

A few minutes later, Annie returned to the porch. In one hand she had a pencil. In the other hand she had four little metal rings.

"Are you ready?" asked Annie.

We all looked at each other. "Um, yes," we said.

First, Annie kneeled in the yard. Then, she carefully stuck the pencil into the ground, so that it was standing straight up.

Next, Annie took one of her little metal rings and slipped it over the pencil.

"Annie," we started to say, "You CANNOT make those little rings float."

"Oh, they will certainly float," said Annie. "These little rings are magnets!"

"So what?" we asked. Magnets were nothing special. Magnets were just little things that you stuck onto the refrigerator door. Magnets were not things that could float.

Annie now took out a second magnet ring. "Okay, everybody watch. I'm going to slip this one onto the pencil too, and it will float – it will hover in the air above the first one. Ready?"

We all watched. We all waited.

Slowly, Annie placed the second magnet onto the pencil – and dropped it.

Quick as a blink, the second magnet slid down the pencil. But instead of falling straight to the ground like

the first one – this magnet bounced back up! There it hung, floating, about an inch above the ground! We all gasped with surprise.

But Annie didn't stop there. She added another ring, and it hung in the air as well, hovering above the others!

"Wow!"

"Holy cow, Annie, how did you do that?"

Annie leaned back and smiled. "It's called magnetic levitation," she said. "All magnets have a north and south pole. And if you push two north poles together (or two south poles) they fight each other – they try to get away. And if you set the magnets up just so, you can suspend them in the air. There are some trains in Europe that use this same idea – the cars and passengers float a couple of inches above the tracks, all because of magnets."

We all marveled over Annie's floating magnets for a moment. Finally, River Babelski asked, "Can you make them do it without the pencil?"

Annie smiled. "No, that we cannot do. It might hurt Samuel Earnshaw's feelings."

We all looked at each other. We looked at Annie. "Who," we asked, "is Samuel Earnshaw?"

"Oh, never mind," said Annie. "But no, you can't take away the pencil or else all the magnets will just flip over on each other and fall down."

For awhile we just stood there and looked at Annie's magnets. We had to admit: Annie was clever.

Very clever.

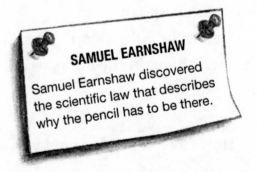

SAMUEL EARNSHAW

Samuel Earnshaw discovered the scientific law that describes why the pencil has to be there.

4.
Annie and the Atoms

*"We must be clear that when it comes to atoms,
language can be used only as in poetry."*
-Niels Bohr, 1885-1962

One happy summer day, we stopped by Annie's house to see if she wanted to go down to the park and play Frisbee. She was sitting on the front steps of her house reading a book and flicking little green bugs away as they climbed up her legs.

"Want to play Frisbee?" we asked.

"I'd come," she said, "but I'm reading about the atom."

We looked over her shoulders at the book.

It was a big, dull-looking book.

And it was full of big, dull-looking words.

"Annie," we said, "that book is horrible. Come, do something fun with us."

"This book," said Annie, "is wonderful. I love atoms."

"What are atoms?" we asked.

"They're very small," said Annie.

"Like your monsters?"

Annie shook her head. "No. Way, way smaller. Too small to see."

"Why don't you use your microscope?"

"They're too small to see even with a microscope. All you can do is read, and think about them. See – " Annie showed us a page – "Everything is made of atoms. All of us, our clothes, our dogs, those trees, that car. Everything is made of them. And they're very fun to learn about."

"Annie," we said, "Listen. You may read big, thick books. And you may be able to find monsters. But you cannot, CANNOT possibly make us believe there is something fun about tiny little specks you can't even see."

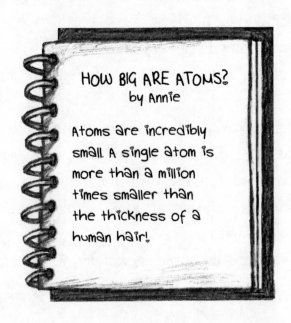

HOW BIG ARE ATOMS?
by Annie

Atoms are incredibly small. A single atom is more than a million times smaller than the thickness of a human hair!

"Come back tomorrow," said Annie, closing the book. "I'll show you then."

* * *

The next day, we stopped by Annie's house once again to see if she had changed her mind about playing Frisbee.

Annie was playing out in the driveway making huge circles in the dirt with a stick. Here's what she'd drawn:

A small circle in the center, with larger circles around that. It looked like a game of some kind. We wandered over.

"Annie," we said, "what is that?"

"A pretend atom," said Annie. "Come here – I'm going to show you how fun they are."

We wandered over. Annie kept talking.

"Atoms are small, but they're made of even smaller pieces. You guys are going to be the smaller pieces." She grabbed five kids and pushed them towards the small center circle. "You five can be the nucleus," she said.

"The what?" we all asked.

"The nucleus – that's the small center part."

The five kids stood loosely in the middle of the circle.

"No!" cried Annie, getting excited, "You're a nucleus, for heaven's sake! You guys are crammed together without any room to move! Squeeze together!"

Giggling, the five kids squeezed together.

"Tighter!" said Annie.

They tried to squeeze tighter, but it was too hard to laugh and squeeze at the same time. The game was just too silly. The nucleus fell apart under its own giggling.

"Hey," said a couple of other kids, "I wanna be in the nucleus, too!"

"No, no," said Annie, pushing them towards the larger circles. "The rest of you guys are electrons. That means you run around the outside on those big paths."

We started to run around the circles.

"Faster!" cried Annie. "Like – as fast as anything you can imagine!"

We ran faster.

"It's not good enough!" shouted Annie through all the laughter. "You're electrons! You're moving so fast around the nucleus that you're just a fuzzy blur! You're everywhere at once!"

Of course, the faster Annie told us to run, the more we laughed, which slowed us down.

Finally, Mary Ann Louis stopped running and said, "I – I'm too tired to run anymore."

"Oh!" cried Annie. "Good. You're running out of energy. When an electron gets tired, it has to jump to a smaller circle."

Mary Ann slowly slinked over to the smaller circle.

"No!" said Annie, jumping into the atom herself. "You have to make a quantum leap! When you're an electron, you're not allowed to touch the space in-between the paths. Like this!"

While she was running at full speed, Annie leapt from one circle to another without touching the dirt in-between.

"How do I get back to a bigger one?" asked Mary Ann, now not tired at all.

"You have to get excited!" said Annie. "When an electron gets excited, it quantum leaps to a bigger circle. And she demonstrated. "Christmas, Christmas, Christmas!" she yelled. (What could be more exciting than thinking about Christmas?) Annie-the-Electron was so excited, she quantum leaped to a bigger circle.

Soon, everyone was quantum leaping from circle to circle. Kyle Materson got into a fight with Macy Fillmore over whose turn it was to stand in the nucleus, but Annie was able to sort it out before Macy began to cry.

We played, laughed, and quantum leaped all afternoon, all the way into the evening until the sun went down and the lights came on, and the mosquitoes started biting us. But then it was time to leave.

"That really was great!" we told Annie. "You were right! Atoms aren't boring after all!"

"No," Annie smiled, brushing the green grass stains off her knees, "but they are a Bohr."

"What's a Bohr?" we all asked.

"Oh, never mind," said Annie.

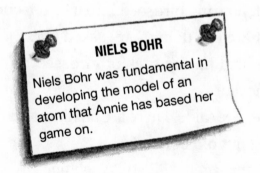

NIELS BOHR

Niels Bohr was fundamental in developing the model of an atom that Annie has based her game on.

5.
Annie Catches a Dinosaur

*"We do not ask for what useful purpose
the birds do sing, for song is their pleasure
since they were created for singing."*
-Johannes Kepler, 1596

One Monday morning towards the end of summer, Annie decided to catch a dinosaur.

We stopped by to see what she was doing. She was in the yard, pouring birdseed into a bird feeder.

"What are you doing?" we asked her.

Annie held up the sack of birdseed. "I'm going to catch a dinosaur."

"Annie," we said. "There are no dinosaurs. Dinosaurs are nothing but old bones."

Annie shrugged. "I'll still catch one."

"YOU CAN'T CATCH A DINOSAUR!" we all cried (although by now, we weren't so sure she couldn't).

Annie ignored us. She finished filling the bird feeder and then carried it to a post in the middle of the yard.

"There," she said.

"There what?" we all asked.

"There's the bird feeder. Now I'm going in. Dad's going to help me memorize the Periodic Table of the Elements."

"What about the dinosaurs?" we asked.

"Oh," said Annie. She looked like she'd already forgotten about them. (How can you forget about catching a dinosaur?) "Oh," she said again. "They probably won't show up for a few days. Come back on Thursday."

On Tuesday, we did nothing. Sometimes we pushed each other on swings and threw Frisbees, but mostly we

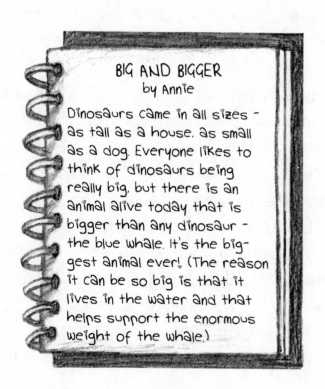

BIG AND BIGGER
by Annie

Dinosaurs came in all sizes — as tall as a house, as small as a dog. Everyone likes to think of dinosaurs being really big, but there is an animal alive today that is bigger than any dinosaur — the blue whale. It's the biggest animal ever! (The reason it can be so big is that it lives in the water and that helps support the enormous weight of the whale.)

just sat around and did nothing – nothing except talk about how smart Annie seemed to be and whether or not we believed that she really would catch a dinosaur. Mary Ann Louis thought she would, and so did River Babelski, so they sat around talking about what weird kinds of dinosaurs Annie would catch.

On Wednesday, we still did nothing. Some of us were getting skeptical ("She ain't gonna find no dino!" shouted Royal Scott), but some of us were confident in Annie ("Oh, yes she will, Royal Scott! You just wait and see!" said Mary Ann).

On Thursday, we ran over to Annie's house early. We ran through the front yard and scared away all the little birds that had gathered around Annie's bird feeder. We rang the doorbell.

Annie answered the door, dressed in her pajamas, looking very sleepy, and eating a bowl of Cheerios. "What do you guys want?" she asked.

"Where are the dinosaurs?!" we asked excitedly. Mary Ann tried to see around Annie, maybe expecting there to be a Diplodocus in the kitchen. "It's Thursday! Have you caught them yet?"

"Oh," said Annie, not excited at all. "Oh, sure, I've got some now." She nodded her head towards the bird feeder. "They're right out there."

We turned. We looked. The little birds were back at

the feeder – sparrows and starlings and chickadees and robins – but no dinosaurs. Not even a lizard.

"Annie," we said. "Those are not dinosaurs. Those are birds."

Annie yawned. "Yeah," she said. "but they are also dinosaur cousins."

"What do you mean, 'dinosaur cousins'?"

Annie took a mouthful of cereal and swallowed it before answering. "Think about birds – they're not like any other animal. They're not mammals because mammals don't lay eggs."

We all agreed; mammals didn't do that. ("What are mammals?" asked Royal Scott. "Dogs and cats and stuff," whispered Mary Ann.)

30

"And birds are not reptiles because birds are warm-blooded. Like dinosaurs," said Annie.

"What's warm-blooded?" we asked.

"Oh, never mind," Annie sighed. "But they stand on two legs – and so did a lot of little dinosaurs."

We all agreed – the similarity was striking.

"And they have scales – on their legs," said Annie. "So did dinosaurs."

"But dinosaurs didn't have feathers," argued River Babelski.

"How do you know?" said Annie.

We were all silent for a time, thinking all this over.

"But," said Annie, "there are a couple things that aren't the same. See, the bones in a bird's tail are short, but dinosaurs had long, bony tails. So that makes them different.

31

Also, birds don't have teeth, but dinosaurs did. So they're not exactly the same things. But, it's fun to think of birds and dinosaurs as kind of cousins – like a dog and a fox, or a lion and a kitten."

"Hey, cool," said Royal Scott. "I'm gonna go home and put up a dinosaur feeder, too!"

"Me too!"

"Me three!"

"Wow," said Mary Ann Louis. Her eyes were shining when she looked at Annie, her hero. "You are a genius, Annie."

Annie blushed modestly and looked at the ground. "Thank you," she said. Behind her, her bowl of Cheerios was only just beginning to grow soggy.

6.
A Piece of Pi

"Mathematics is the language with which
God has written the universe."
-Galileo Galilei, 1564-1642

One afternoon, when the autumn sun was shining down happily, we were all playing outside in Annie's driveway. Some of us were playing hopscotch in the dirt; a couple of us were tossing a basketball back and forth. A few kids were trying to catch falling leaves. Annie was sitting on the steps reading. And Arren Wells was singing "The Song that Never Ends."

After many minutes, Mary Ann Louis asked him to stop.

But he wouldn't. "...This is the song that never ends..."

"It's dumb!" cried Mary Ann.

"...it just goes on and on, my friend."

"Stop it!" said Mary Ann. She covered her ears. "It's silly! You can't sing forever! Even if you sing all day, you'll just have to stop at night to go to bed! Nothing just goes on and on like that."

Annie perked up just then. "Actually," she said, "there is infinity."

Everybody stopped to listen. Even Arren.

Annie crouched in the driveway. With a stick, she drew this pattern in the sand:

"That," she said, "is infinity."

"That," we said, "is a doodle in the dirt."

Annie sighed. "Yes," she said, "but it is also the sign for infinity. That is a math word. It means, 'a number that has no end.'"

("It looks like the number eight tipped over," said Earl James.)

"Okay," said Mary Ann. "So that's infinity. What does that have to do with Arren's ridiculous song?"

"You said, 'nothing just goes on and on.' Well — some numbers do. Like infinity. And like Pi."

So of course we had to ask. "Annie," we said, "What is Pi?"

("My favorite dessert," somebody giggled.)

"Here it is," said Annie, drawing another pattern:

We all admired Annie's fine design.

"Pi is a number that gets stuck," said Annie. "It just runs over itself, on and on, forever. Here, I'll show you."

"Annie – " we said, " – you said you were a scientist. What are you doing playing with math?"

"Math is a science," said Annie. "Now look. Take, for example, a circle..."

(She drew a small circle in the sand.)

"And now take a tape measure..."

(She got a tape measure from the garage.)

"And measure the distance across the circle. See? Four inches."

"Annie," we said, "WHO CARES?"

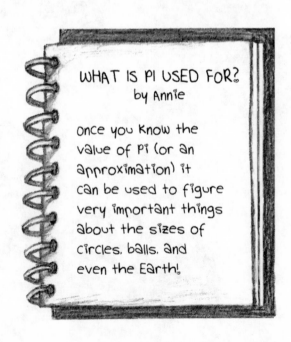

WHAT IS PI USED FOR?
by Annie

Once you know the value of Pi (or an approximation) it can be used to figure very important things about the sizes of circles, balls, and even the Earth!

"You watch!" said Annie. "It's a puzzle! Now, take some kite string, and cut it into four-inch pieces."

We watched while Annie did that.

"Now," said Annie, "here's the BIG QUESTION: How many four-inch strings does it take to go around the outside of my circle?"

Nobody said anything. What was the point of this?

"Well, let's see," said Annie. She laid them out. "Four inches, four inches, four inches, and...ta da!"

We all looked. It took three strings to go around the outside of the circle.

Except they didn't quite fit. There was a small gap left over, too small for another string, but too wide to be ignored.

"And that," said Annie, "is how Pi gets stuck. It takes three, plus a little bit extra. But no matter what you do, you can never exactly figure out how much extra. If you are clever with circles and try to do that math, you just get a number which never ends."

Annie wrote in the dirt:

3.1415965...

"See?" she said. "It will just go on and on. Nobody – not even Archimedes – can figure out the end."

"Who," we asked, "is Archimedes?"

"Oh, never mind," said Annie. "Anyway, it goes on and on and on. Now Arren, please continue with that beautiful song." And Annie looked up sweetly.

But Arren had become bored and had wandered off by the swing set. All was quiet once again.

"Thank you!" Mary Ann whispered to Annie. She started to erase Annie's circles with her shoe.

"You're welcome," said Annie. "But please, do not disturb my circles."

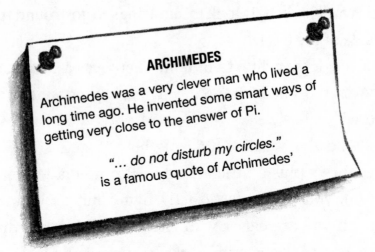

ARCHIMEDES

Archimedes was a very clever man who lived a long time ago. He invented some smart ways of getting very close to the answer of Pi.

"... do not disturb my circles." is a famous quote of Archimedes'

7.
No Time Like The Present

"You can show black is white by argument," said Filby, "but you will never convince me."
-H.G. Wells, *The Time Machine* , 1895

"Yesterday, I fell off my bike," Mary Ann Louis was saying. She pointed to a scrape on her elbow. "Look what happened!"

We all agreed that was really too bad. "What happened?" we asked.

"I was coming down the driveway," Mary Ann told us, "and a silly squirrel came running out in front of me. When I tried to stop fast, my wheels started to slide on some sand, and I tipped over. It hurt A LOT!"

It didn't really look like it hurt a lot, but we were sympathetic anyway.

"You know," said Royal Scott, "that reminds me of this movie I saw on TV the other night. It was where this scientist guy left his car parked on the side of a hill, and while he wasn't looking, it rolled down the hill and fell into a lake."

"What," we all asked, "does that have to do with Mary Ann's elbow?"

"Well you see," said Royal, "the car was worth a lot of money, and it was ruined. So the scientist guy built himself a time machine, and he went back in time to earlier that morning and parked his car up on a flat place instead. Then his car was saved."

We all agreed that was quite clever of him.

"Maybe," Royal told Mary Ann, "you could go back in time and decide not to ride your bike! Then your arm wouldn't be hurt. Of course, you would have to find someone who could build you a time machine..."

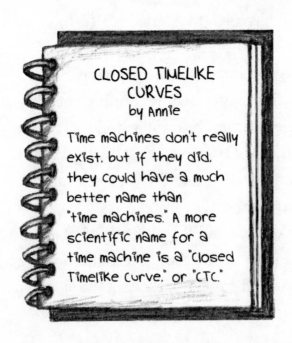

CLOSED TIMELIKE
CURVES
by Annie

Time machines don't really exist, but if they did, they could have a much better name than "time machines." A more scientific name for a time machine is a "Closed Timelike Curve," or "CTC."

We all turned to Annie.

"Oh, no!" said Annie. "You guys don't think I'm really a scientist, remember?"

"Oh, please try, Annie!" begged Mary Ann. "It would be such a charming experiment!"

"Yeah, Annie!" said Arren Wells. "If you can do it, then...we'll believe you and say you're a scientist."

We all waited for what Annie would say.

After a moment, Annie shook her head. "No one," she said, "can build a time machine that travels backwards, into the past."

"Why not?" we cried. "You've done all kinds of things! Why can't you do this?"

Annie sat down on the front steps. "Okay, I can prove to you that this is impossible. But you have to really pay attention because it's all about thinking, and I don't want to have to explain it twice."

We sat down.

Annie began. "If you went back in time to yesterday and stopped yourself from riding the bike, then you wouldn't have fallen and scraped your elbow, and we wouldn't be sitting here right now talking about going back in time to stop yourself from riding the bike and scraping your elbow. The fact that we're talking about it proves that you in fact didn't do it." Finishing, Annie smiled.

We didn't say anything. It took a few minutes to figure out exactly what Annie had just said. Some of us didn't get it at all.

"But," said Annie, "traveling into the future might be possible. If you could build a spaceship that travelled, very very fast, you could sort of go into the future more quickly than someone who didn't go on the trip with you. But that isn't really 'time travelling' in the way that you're talking about."

Everyone was quiet for awhile, and you could hear that simple silence that comes when people are thinking.

"It would be something," said Annie, "if time traveling in the way you're talking about were possible." Her eyes got far away and dreamy. "Then we could all go far into the future and meet Weena."

We all looked at Annie. "Who," we said, "IS WEENA?!"

Annie laughed. She leaned back on the steps, resting in the sunshine. "Oh," she giggled, "Oh, never mind."

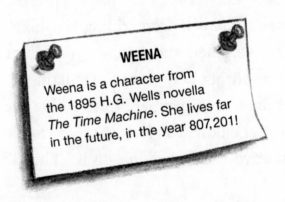

WEENA

Weena is a character from the 1895 H.G. Wells novella *The Time Machine*. She lives far in the future, in the year 807,201!

8.
Water, Water

"But still try, for who knows what is possible..."
-Michael Faraday, 1870

One cold, windy afternoon in late fall, as the sun was setting, we were all walking home from playing in the park. Royal Scott was tossing a football back and forth with Oliver Sloane. Macy Fillmore was whining about how hard her schoolwork was. Annie was humming a little song that had something to do with memorizing Newton's laws of motion. And Arnold Baxter was waving and calling us over to his yard.

"Hey!" he yelled. "I need help." We wandered over.

Arnold was standing near his little fruit trees. He had four of them – an apple, a pear, a plum, and a cherry. His fruit trees were his favorite things in the whole world – he tended them all year long, waiting for the fruit to come.

"What's wrong?" we all asked.

Arnold was holding an apple with one bite taken out of it. He pointed to it. "They're still too tart to pick," he said. "They need a few more days. But the weather says it's going to get really cold tonight. The fruit will be ruined!"

We all looked around. There certainly were plenty of nice-looking apples, pears, plums, and cherries. "What a shame," we said. Annie, who was looking at the fruit very carefully, said nothing.

"I know!" said Earl James. "We'll build a huge bonfire in the yard, with ten-foot flames, and keep in running all night long! That'll put out enough heat to keep the fruit warm."

"Yeah!" agreed Mary Ann Louis. "We can sing songs and roast marshmallows!"

Arnold frowned. "I don't think we can do that in my yard. Mom hates smoke, and I'm sure it would break some town rule."

"Maybe we could wrap the trees with blankets," somebody suggested.

"Yeah," said Arnold, "but that would be an awful lot of blankets." He looked up; the trees were several feet taller than he was. "I'm not even sure we could do it if we wanted to."

We all agreed it looked hopeless. Arnold's fruit was going to be ruined for sure.

Suddenly, Annie snapped her fingers. We all jumped.

"WHAT?" we asked.

"I think," said Annie, "we should water the trees. Do you have a hose nearby?"

Nobody said anything. That made NO sense. ("I knew she wasn't a scientist!" whispered Kyle Materson.)

"Or a bucket?" said Annie again.

"Annie," said Arnold, "I don't see how watering the trees is going to help at all..."

"Oh, it will certainly help," said Annie, smiling. She had that clever look on her face again – where her eyes seemed to be giggling.

Arnold flashed us a "beats me" look and turned on the hose.

Annie took the hose and watered the trees. She watered, watered, and watered. It kept getting darker, and colder out. House lights started coming on, glowing in the dusk. Still Annie watered on.

Finally she threw down the hose. "There!" she said. "That will keep the fruit from freezing."

We looked at the trees. We looked at the wet ground. We looked at Annie, whose breath was visible from the cold, and looked golden in the glow of the house.

"Annie," we said, "you didn't do anything. You just watered the trees."

Annie sighed. "You guys never believe me."

"It's just that – "

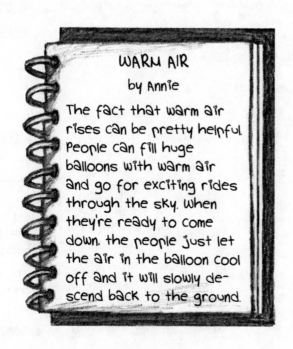

WARM AIR
by Annie

The fact that warm air rises can be pretty helpful. People can fill huge balloons with warm air and go for exciting rides through the sky. When they're ready to come down, the people just let the air in the balloon cool off and it will slowly descend back to the ground.

"– tonight," Annie interrupted, "all of this water – " (she gestured all around) "– will freeze. But for water to freeze, all of its own warmth has to go someplace. It goes up into the air. And warm air likes to float upwards. And that warm air will rise up around the trees, and protect the fruit from the cold."

"It will?" asked Arnold, brightening.

"Oh yes, it certainly will," said Annie. "I have studied these things – you have not."

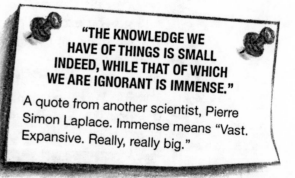

"I HAVE STUDIED THESE THINGS – YOU HAVE NOT."
A quote of Isaac Newton's.

Amy Sheldon was skeptical. "I don't know, Annie. I've never heard anything like that before..."

Annie smiled. "The knowledge we have of things is small indeed, while that of which we are ignorant is immense."

"What?" said Amy.

"Oh, never mind," said Annie.

(And the next week, we all enjoyed fine fruit from Arnold's trees.)

"THE KNOWLEDGE WE HAVE OF THINGS IS SMALL INDEED, WHILE THAT OF WHICH WE ARE IGNORANT IS IMMENSE."
A quote from another scientist, Pierre Simon Laplace. Immense means "Vast. Expansive. Really, really big."

9.
Annie is Worth Her Salt

*"Every Planet therefore must have its own
Waters of such a temper not liable to Frost."*
-Christaan Huygens, 1698

One day, in the middle of winter, we all decided to go sledding. We stopped by Annie's house to tell her. She was out in the yard trying to look at snowflakes with a magnifying glass.

"Annie," we said, "want to go sledding?"

"Sure," said Annie, putting the magnifying glass in her pocket. "I'll come."

The sledding hill was at the park. Most of the park was closed in the winter because it was too cold and boring to play on swings or slides in the snow. But the sledding hill was free to play on all the time.

Earl James was the first one to try it. He got on the sled with his little brother, Leroy. They shot down the hill. Everything was fine, until the very end, when it was time to stop. The problem was that they couldn't. Earl

James tried to put his feet out to stop the sled, but he just kept going – slipping and sliding and yelling. Finally, he and Leroy smashed into a huge snowbank. POOF!

We all came running to see if they were okay.

"Look – look what happened to us!" Earl James squealed. "I'm not doing that again."

We all agreed. Nobody wanted to crash into the snow bank.

"There's even rocks behind there," said Amy Sheldon with a shiver.

"Guess we'll all have to go home," we said. "Right, Annie?"

But Annie wasn't listening. She was walking over the path that Earl James and Leroy had made. She was studying the wild footprints of Earl James' feet when they had been trying to stop. She was thinking.

"I see the problem," she said. "There is pure ice underneath this little dusting of snow." As if to prove her point, her left foot started to slip even while she was standing there. But she didn't fall.

We all came to look. A couple of kids slipped and did fall. It sure was icy.

"We'll have to forget it," someone said. Everyone agreed.

Except Annie.

"No," she said. "I think we should be able to fix this."

"Annie," we said, "you are smart. You've found monsters, and dinosaurs, and numbers that have no end. But you cannot, CANNOT make the ice melt."

Annie shrugged.

"Well, the ice isn't just going to melt by itself!" somebody said.

"No, it sure isn't," said Annie, " – at least, not without violating the second law of thermodynamics."

We sighed. "Annie," we said, "What on earth is the – "

"Oh, never mind," said Annie. "But let's think about this. What causes ice to melt?"

We thought. "Sunshine?" somebody asked.

"Sure," said Annie, "but I can't make the sun shine."

"Besides," said Earl James, "even the sun won't make ice melt in the winter. It's still too cold."

Annie smiled.

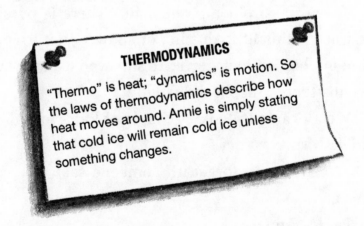

THERMODYNAMICS

"Thermo" is heat; "dynamics" is motion. So the laws of thermodynamics describe how heat moves around. Annie is simply stating that cold ice will remain cold ice unless something changes.

"You're not thinking of making the park warmer?" we asked.

"No," said Annie, "I'm thinking of using chemistry to make the ice melt at a lower temperature."

"WHAT?!?" we all screamed. Chemistry was for people in labs who mixed colorful liquids together. Chemistry was not for melting ice in parks. "Annie, you CANNOT use chemistry in a park."

"Come back tomorrow," said Annie. "I'll show you then."

We started to leave.

"Oh, and," she called one more time, "bring some salt."

* * *

The next day, we all met at the park once again. Nothing had changed. It was still winter. It was still cold. And the bottom of the hill was still covered in ice.

The only thing different was Annie. She was standing at the bottom of the hill. And she was smiling.

"Did everyone bring some salt?" she asked.

We nodded. Everyone handed over a salt shaker. Some of them had been hard to get. Not everyone's mom had wanted to give up their salt for no reason. ("I don't know, Mom. Annie wants it.")

Annie took all the salt. She herself had brought a huge can of it. She was serious.

She had already scraped away the snow on top of the ice. Now it was just a big slippery hard place. Very carefully, Annie walked out to the middle.

"Now," she announced, opening the first shaker, "to melt the ice!" And she sprinkled the salt all over the ice.

At first there was nothing, but then, slowly, came the noise. The ice started to crackle.

The noise got louder, and faster. Crackle-Crackle-Crackle-Crackle-Crackle! It was like Rice Krispies. Annie was melting the ice!

"Annie!" we cried. "It's working!"

But Annie didn't stop there. One after another, she opened all the other salt shakers and poured salt every-where – until it was all over the ice.

We looked closer – you could even see the ice melting! Slowly, the salt was grabbing ice and turning it back into water.

"Annie!" we said. "How did you know?"

Annie smiled.

"It is just a little chemistry," she said. "Ice happens when water gets too tired. The water is tired because it's cold. And all of these tiny bits of water stop moving around, because they're tired. They turn hard as a rock. But," and she held up an empty salt shaker, "when salt grabs onto the tiny bits of water, it helps them to stay moving around. It helps them to not be tired. And if they're not tired, they're not ice."

Soon, the ice had melted enough to be safe. And we all took turns sledding down the hill.

"Wow!" we all said later, at the end of the day when we were out of breath from laughing and playing. "Great job, Annie!"

"Thank you," said Annie, taking a low bow. Then she slipped on a little patch of ice that had been missed and toppled over.

SNOWFLAKES
by Annie

Snowflakes come in lots of shapes, but they all have six sides (unless one is damaged during its fall from the cloud). This six-sided shape is known as a "hexagon."

10.
Annie and the Four Moons

*"If I have seen further, it is only by standing
on the shoulders of giants."*

-Isaac Newton, 1676

One day, very early in the spring, when the days were still short and chilly, we stopped by Annie's house to see if she wanted to go splash through mud puddles with us.

"Sure," said Annie. "I won't be busy until late tonight."

"What," we asked, "are you doing late tonight?"

Annie was putting on her sweater as she shut the front door. "I'm going out in the dark – to see four moons, all at one time."

We looked at each other. Annie had to be wrong this time. EVERYONE knows there is only ONE moon.

We looked at Annie. She was humming and watching the blooming crocuses.

"Annie," we said, "there is only one moon. Not four. You may be able to find a monster, and you may be able to make magnets float, and you may be able to have fun with atoms, and you may be able to compare birds to dinosaurs, and you may be able to use chemistry to melt ice in a park, BUT YOU CANNOT SEE FOUR MOONS AT ONCE! THERE IS ONLY ONE MOON!"

Annie shrugged. "Won't you guys ever believe me?" she asked.

We thought about that. We thought during the walk to the park. We thought while we looked for puddles. We thought while we all ran around giggling, splashing in the puddles.

And this is what we thought:

Maybe Annie is a scientist.

She had always done exactly what she said she would do. So maybe...

EARTH'S MOON –
A MOON WITH
A REAL NAME
by Annie

Earth's moon has a real name. One that's a lot better than "Earth's moon." It's called "Luna." The sun has a real name, too: "Sol."

After we finished playing, we asked Annie: "When will you see the four moons?"

"Tonight," said Annie, "after dark. Here in the park. Does anyone want to come?"

* * *

The day dragged slowly. The days always dragged slowly when we were waiting for Annie to do something.

We were bored all afternoon, all evening, all through dinner, all after dinner. It took FOREVER for the sun to set. Finally, it was dark.

We gathered up flashlights. We put on jackets. And we headed for the park.

Annie was already there. But she had a special flashlight – one that gave off red light. Annie called us over.

"Turn off those white flashlights," she called, trying to cover her eyes with her arm. "When you look at stars, you should use a red flashlight – red light is easier on your eyes at night."

Annie was standing in the middle of the park. She had a little telescope with three legs set up.

"Annie," we said, "will that telescope really work?"

"Oh, yes," said Annie. "It will certainly work."

We waited. Annie waited. Nothing moved. Finally we said:

"Annie, what are we waiting for?"

Annie smiled, her face lit up by her red flashlight.

"We're waiting for that big cloud to move," she said. And she pointed. The sky was mostly clear, with lots of stars, but there was one big cloud.

"What we need to see is behind it;" said Annie. "But come on; there's lots to do in the meantime."

Annie laid down in the grass, with her hands under her head. "Try it, guys," she said.

We all laid down in the grass.

It was pretty dark, and kind of cold, but very special. Annie turned off her flashlight, leaving us in the dark. There were simply stars everywhere.

Pretty soon: "What's the name of that star, Annie?"

"Altair."

"And that one?"

"Vega."

Suddenly, a bright streak whizzed across the sky! It lasted for just a moment, and then its shadow slowly faded away.

"That," we said, "was a shooting star!"

"That," said Annie, "was a meteor."

Just then, the big cloud finally moved out of the way. Annie stood up, brushed herself off, and went to the telescope.

We all gathered around. And we waited.

SHOOTING STARS AND METEORS

Shooting stars and meteors are the same thing. A "shooting star" is the common, unscientific name; a "meteor" is its real name. They aren't "stars" at all, but tiny pebbles or specks of dust that fall from space and streak so fast through our air that they light up. Once in a while, a bigger meteor will make it all the way to the ground and become a "meteorite."

Annie put her eye to the telescope. She wiggled it, slowly. Back and forth. Back and forth.

"Annie," we said, "what are you looking for?"

Annie took her eye off the telescope for a moment, and pointed to a very bright star. "We're going to look at Jupiter."

"YOU SAID WE WERE GOING TO SEE FOUR MOONS AT ONCE!" we all exclaimed in the dark.

"We are," said Annie.

Finally, Annie finished positioning the telescope. Then, she backed away carefully.

"All right," she said. "Now, each of you take turns looking through the telescope – but be very careful not to bump it."

And then:

"Goodness!"

"Wow!"

"Hey, neat!"

Inside the telescope, you could see the planet Jupiter! It was very pretty.

"But," we asked Annie, "WHAT ABOUT THE FOUR MOONS?"

"Look very carefully," said Annie. "In a straight line, to the left and right of Jupiter. You will see four little pinpricks of light."

We all looked. And once again, we all gasped.

"Annie!" we cried. "Are those – "

" – Moons of Jupiter," said Annie. "Jupiter actually has a whole bunch of moons – but those four are big enough to see with a little telescope. If you look again tomorrow, they will all have changed positions."

We couldn't deny it anymore. We all backed away from the telescope. "Annie," we said, "you are simply amazing. You are a scientist!"

Annie smiled in the dark – you could hardly see her. But she was smiling. She began to take down the telescope. "Thank you," she whispered. "But looking through this telescope isn't really a big deal. I mean, it's not like it's the view from Voyager 1 or 2. But still, it means a lot to hear you guys say that. It's almost like hearing those words coming from Galileo himself."

And once again, we had to ask:

"Annie, what is Voyager 1 or 2? Who is Galileo?"

Annie laughed. We heard her voice, but it was too dark to see. She was like a shadow, lost in the night. But the laugh in her voice bounced across the lawn, touched our ears, and faded away into the distance:

"Oh," she said, "oh, never mind..."

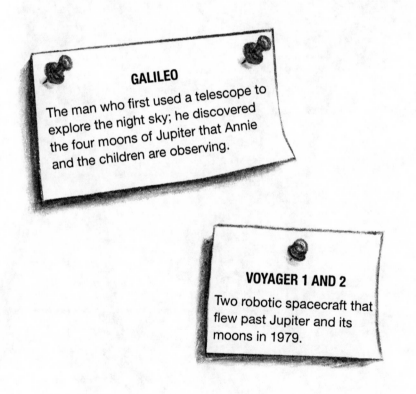

GALILEO

The man who first used a telescope to explore the night sky; he discovered the four moons of Jupiter that Annie and the children are observing.

VOYAGER 1 AND 2

Two robotic spacecraft that flew past Jupiter and its moons in 1979.

11.
Annie the Artist?

The next day, we ran over to Annie's house. She wasn't outside. She wasn't downstairs. We asked Annie's mom.

"I don't know what she's up to now," Annie's mom said with a sigh. "She just disappeared upstairs with glue and paper and paint – goodness, I hope she doesn't make a mess like the time she tried to turn her bedroom into a planetarium..."

We dashed upstairs. We ran to Annie's room. And we all gasped.

Annie was sitting in the middle of the room. She was wearing a filthy painter's smock. The smock was covered in color. So was Annie.

All around the room, Annie had taped up big pieces of paper and poster board. And she had obviously been painting for quite a while. She'd painted all kinds of pictures: trees, people, her cat, a door.

"What," we said, "ARE YOU DOING?"

Annie smiled. There was paint all over her face. "I am an artist."

"You said you were a scientist!" we all shouted.

Annie shrugged.

"I've been studying art lately," she said. "Here, look at this book." The name of the book was Art Through the Ages. "Here is Di Vinci's The Last Supper," she said, turning to a page. "And here's Renoir's Girl with a Hoop. I'm trying to become an artist, as well. Not just painting. There's also music, sculpture, literature, theater, photography, poetry...there are just so many different kinds of art..."

Author's Notes

Hurray! You finished the book! Now you can put it down and go ride your bike, or play with the dog, or do whatever it is you do when you're not reading.

OR....!

You can read the next part of this book. It isn't required; you don't have to read it. In fact, you may have already read parts of it on Annie's notes, throughout the book. But if you were inspired by Annie's science and would like to know a little more, then you might enjoy this next portion.

I'm going to explain a bit more about some of the things that happened in the story, chapter by chapter, and I'm also going to try to explain a bit more about the things Annie says. Annie doesn't always make herself completely clear – she often starts to explain something complicated and then stops. I'll see if I can help sort things out...but with Annie, who knows?

-d.j.

Chapter 1, A New Girl

- *"I'm a scientist."* A scientist is someone who assumes there must be an ordered and predictable way that the world works and uses careful study and observation to figure out what those ways are.

- *"NO KID CAN BE A SCIENTIST."* The children have obviously never heard of Mary Anning. You might want to learn more about her.

Chapter 2, Annie Discovers a Monster

- *"The name of the book was Biology."* Biology is the study of living things – plants, animals, cells, etc...

- *"There is a monster in Loch Ness"* Loch Ness is a large lake in Scotland that is supposedly the home of a famous sea creature, although this has never been proven. (I think Annie is kidding!)

- *"...her geology samples."* Geology is the study of rocks.

- *"I ♥ Protein Molecules"* Remember, Annie is studying biology. That might give you a hint as to what a protein molecule is. As to where Annie got the boots, I have no idea.

- *"Over in a corner of the room was a microscope..."* A microscope is an amazingly fun tool. It lets you look at very, very tiny things really, really close up. Kind of like binoculars. Only backwards.

- *"... microorganisms."* What a scary word. But it's not really that hard. An organism is just a fancy word for something that is alive. Micro just means "small." So a microorganism is "small life."

- *"Robert Hooke would be so pleased..."* Robert Hooke was an English scientist who first used the word cell to describe the building blocks of life.

Chapter 3, Magnetic Levitation

• *"...a big picture taken from space, showing the whole planet Earth just sitting there in the blackness, hanging on nothing."* The photograph Annie is showing them is NASA photo AS17-148-22727, or "The Blue Marble," which was taken by the Apollo 17 astronauts while on their way to visit the moon. You can see it here: *http://spaceflight.nasa.gov/gallery/images/ apollo/apollo17/html/as17-148-22727.html*

• *"It's called magnetic levitation"* It just means that the only thing holding up the object is a magnetic field.

• *"It might hurt Samuel Earnshaw's feelings."* Samuel Earnshaw discovered the scientific law that describes why the pencil has to be there...Annie is making a joke, I think.

Chapter 4, Annie and the Atoms

- *"...I'm reading about the atom."* To figure out what an atom is, imagine taking a piece of bread and cutting it in half. Then you cut one of the halves in half. Then you cut that piece in half. Then you cut that piece in half. Then you cut that piece in half. And you keep doing that for as long as you can. After about a bazillion cuts (okay, more like 80 or 90), you might get down to the smallest possible piece – that is an atom. (You can't really do this – atoms are too small and the knife wouldn't be sharp enough anyway.)

- *"You're everywhere at once!"* In what has got to be among the strangest aspects of nature, electrons are both a particle, and a wave, AT THE SAME TIME. So an electron is a speck, and an electron is also not a speck, but just a thing that exists, like the wind. Weird.

- *"...they are a Bohr."* A play-on-words. Niels Bohr was fundamental in developing the model of an atom that Annie has based her game on. Why she can't just play hopscotch, I have no idea.

Chapter 5, Annie Catches a Dinosaur

• *"...Periodic Table of the Elements."* What is this? Do you think it fits with Annie's personality? It must be left over from Annie's studies of atoms in Chapter 4.

• *"...maybe expecting there to be a Diplodocus in the kitchen."* I'm not going to tell you what a Diplodocus looked like – you'll have to find out on your own. (But I bet you know, already!)

• *"What's warm-blooded?"* Being warm-blooded means that an animal can produce and maintain its own body temperature. For instance, a dog or a cat's body is always warm, even if it is outside in a cold, wintery environment. Other animals, like snakes and lizards and turtles, are cold-blooded, which means their body temperature is controlled by the air around them. You can sometimes find a snake warming itself in the sunlight – it does this to raise its body temperature. If a cold-blooded animal gets too cold, it will quickly become tired and sluggish. Annie is suggesting that dinosaurs were active animals – like birds.

Chapter 6, A Piece of Pi

- *"...there is infinity."* In math, the idea of "infinity" is that you just sort of pretend that this "number" has an unlimited value. Strange. Surprisingly, this almost pretend number can be very useful in solving very difficult math problems.

- *"And like Pi."* Pi is the circumference of a circle divided by its diameter. It's a math problem that has given trouble to many, many people for thousands and thousands of years.

- *"...not even Archimedes...can figure out the end."* Archimedes was a very clever man who lived a long time ago. He invented some smart ways of getting very close to the answer of Pi.

- *"...do not disturb my circles."* A famous quote of Archimedes'. I have no idea where Annie heard it.

Chapter 7, No Time Like The Present

- *"It would be such a charming experiment!"* A real scientific experiment involves taking careful measurements, then changing something, and then re-taking the measurements to find out if what you did made any difference. Mary Ann has misused the term slightly.

- *"If you went back in time to yesterday, and stopped yourself from riding the bike..."* Annie's argument here is known as the "Grandfather Paradox." It basically means that if you are the effect of something, it doesn't make any sense for you to be able to go back and prevent your own cause. What do you think? Might there be any way around the Grandfather Paradox? If so, what might that way be?

- *"If you could build a spaceship that travelled very very fast..."* This type of "time travel" is called "time dilation," and is a consequence of Albert Einstein's Special Theory of Relativity – which is a very long name for a very complicated scientific theory. It only works if an object travels very close to the speed of light. The Special Theory of Relativity describes many strange effects such as this. How Annie is aware of it is anybody's guess.

- *"'Who,' we said, 'IS WEENA?!'"* Weena is a character from the 1895 H.G. Wells novella *The Time Machine*. She lives far in the future, in the year 807,201!

Chapter 8, Water, Water

- *"...Newton's laws of motion."* These are Isaac Newton's classical, basic laws that can explain how stuff moves around – everything from rocks to rockets. (I think the talk about time travel got Annie thinking about physics.) Put very simply and sort of sloppily, they are:

1. If something is moving, it keeps moving. Forever. Unless something stops it. And if it something is still, it stays still. Forever. Unless something moves it.

2. It takes a certain amount of energy to move something or to stop it from moving.

3. If something moves, it tends to move something else in the exact opposite way. Whew! Who would want to memorize all that?

- *"I have studied these things – you have not."* A quote of Newton's.

- *"The knowledge we have of things is small indeed, while that of which we are ignorant is immense."* Another quote from another scientist, Pierre Simon Laplace. Immense means "Vast. Expansive. Really, really big."

Chapter 9, Annie is Worth Her Salt

• *"...not without violating the second law of thermody-namics."* "Thermo" is heat; "dynamics" is motion. So the laws of thermodynamics describe how heat moves around. Annie is simply stating that cold ice will remain cold ice unless something changes.

Chapter 10, Annie and the Four Moons

- *"...watching the blooming crocuses."* I bet you can find out what a crocus is. I'll give you a hint. It's a plant. And it's not a bush.

- *"...a little telescope"* A telescope is so cool. It lets you look close up at things that are terribly far away. Like planets. And moons. Annie sure has a lot of nice equipment.

- *"...a shooting star!...a meteor."* These are the same thing. A "shooting star" is the common, unscientific name; a "meteor" is its real name. They aren't "stars" at all, but tiny pebbles or specks of dust that fall from space and streak so fast through our air that they light up. Once in a while, a bigger meteor will make it all the way to the ground, and become a "meteorite."

- *"...be very careful not to bump it."* Telescopes are very finicky, and it's quite easy to knock them off of your subject.

• *"...Voyager 1 or 2"* Two robotic spacecraft that flew past Jupiter and its moons in 1979.

• *"...Galileo"* The man who first used a telescope to explore the night sky; he discovered the four moons of Jupiter that Annie and the children are observing.

A note to parents

Some of the science ideas presented in this book may seem far beyond the traditional grade level of the children reading it. That's okay! Even if the child doesn't grasp the nuances and details of an idea, it's still quite beneficial to be exposed to these words and thoughts at a young age. Later in their educations, the kids will be presented with these concepts "for real," and – hopefully – they'll remember and think: "Hey! I've heard of this before...it was in that book..."

You can also keep up to date with Annie by liking the Annie the Scientist Facebook page at *www.facebook.com/AnnieTheScientist*

About the Author

When he was a kid, Daniel Johnson did some of the things Annie does in this story. He had his very own telescope, and he spent plenty of time playing with magnets and batteries. He found a fossil once. He didn't, however, own a microscope, and he knew nothing about the interiors of atoms until he was a lot older. He did try (rather unsuccessfully) to build a time machine on several occasions. Today Dan is a photographer and also writes books for kids. Someday Dan hopes to have a pet emu.

About the Illustrator

As a kid, Lynn excelled more in art than in science class. She could usually be found lost in another world reading or drawing. She particularly loved to draw Sunday comic strips and album covers. (This was way before the internet and CDs!)

Lynn still spends countless hours getting lost in other worlds through reading, drawing and writing stories.

CPSIA information can be obtained at www.ICGtesting.com
Printed in the USA
LVOW08*2111201113

362178LV00003B/3/P